BELLA'S CHOCOLATE SURPRISE

ADAM GUILLAIN & ELKE STEINER

MILET

Milet Publishing, LLC
333 North Michigan Avenue
Suite 530
Chicago, IL 60601
Email info@milet.com
Website www.milet.com

First published by Milet Publishing, LLC in 2007

Copyright © 2007 by Adam Guillain for text
Copyright © 2007 by Elke Steiner for illustrations
Copyright © 2007 by Milet Publishing, LLC

ISBN 978 1 84059 505 5

Printed on paper from sustainable forests.

Printed in China by 1010 Printning International Ltd.

Please see our website www.milet.com for more
titles featuring Bella Balistica.

BELLA'S CHOCOLATE SURPRISE

ADAM GUILLAIN & ELKE STEINER

"Fair Trade chocolate means a lot to our farmers. It opens the doors to development and gives children access to healthcare, education, and a decent standard of living."

K. Ohemeng-Tinyase, Managing Director
of Kuapa Kokoo cocoa cooperative, Ghana

Bella Balistica was born in Guatemala and now lives with Annie, her adoptive mother, in London. She discovers a magical pendant that had once belonged to her Guatemalan birthmother and is instantly connected with her animal twin – the resplendent Quetzal bird – and her adventures begin . . .

"Can I go and play football in the park?" Bella asked her mum.

Annie had just finished preparing Bella's birthday cake for her party the next day.

"Yes," said Annie, "but first you need to help me clear away the table."

"But that will take ages," Bella sighed.

"The quicker you help me, the sooner you'll get to the park," said Annie.

"You're late," said Charlie. "And you've got chocolate on your face."

"I had to help Mum tidy up," Bella complained, wiping away the chocolate.

Charlie gave Bella a knowing look. "My mum wouldn't let me come out till I tidied my bedroom," she grumbled.

When she got home from the park, Bella took the last chocolate chip cookie from the tin and went straight upstairs to the attic.

"Now, where are you . . . ?" she muttered, taking her jewellery box from an old Guatemalan chest and carefully unlocking its secret compartment. Bella's eyes twinkled with joy as she took out the magical pendant that had once belonged to her Guatemalan birthmother. It was the pendant that gave Bella her powers and connected her with her animal twin.

The moment she slipped it on, there was a sharp tapping at the skylight.

"Any cookie for me?" squawked the Quetzal when Bella opened the window to let him in. Bella broke the chocolate chip cookie in half.

"Chocolate," smiled Bella, licking her lips. "It must be the most delicious food in the entire world."

"Any idea where it comes from?" asked the Quetzal.
"The shops," said Bella.
The Quetzal sighed and shook his head. "Fetch me the globe," he tutted.

"Much of the world's best chocolate comes from Ghana, in West Africa," said the Quetzal, pointing with his beak. "You do know chocolate is made from a fruit called cacao?"

"From a fruit!" cried Bella. "You're joking."

"Follow me," said the Quetzal.

"Where are we going?" Bella asked.

"To Ghana, of course," said the Quetzal, turning to fly.

Bella was soon up and out of the skylight, flying after her colourful friend.

"Do you know what presents you're getting for your birthday?" asked the Quetzal.

"Yes," said Bella. "I wrote a list."

The Quetzal rolled his eyes. "No surprises then," he mumbled.

"Not unless I get everything I asked for," said Bella.

Using the power of the pendant, and with the Quetzal as her guide, Bella was soon flying over a bustling city port.

"Wow!" she exclaimed. "I love exciting cities."

"Tough," squawked the Quetzal. "We're headed for the countryside."

Bella and the Quetzal landed in a clearing in the middle of a large forest.

"What are all these children doing?" Bella asked.

"Helping their mums," said the Quetzal.

Bella felt bad. "I thought we were here to find out about chocolate?" she said.

"We are," said the Quetzal. "Maybe you could start by helping with the cacao harvest this morning."

At first Bella found the local children were a little suspicious of her.

"What are you doing here?" asked one of the older boys.

"I'd like to help with the harvest," Bella replied.

"Then you're more than welcome," said the boy.
"My name's Michael. Me and my sister, Esther, will show you what to do."

Bella was surprised by how hard all the children worked, helping their parents without ever complaining.

"But where's the chocolate?" Bella asked Esther and Michael, as she stared inside a broken pod.

"It's the beans inside that make the chocolate," Esther laughed.

"After we pick the fruit, we open the pods and scoop out all the pulp," added Michael.

"Then we put them in piles and cover them with banana leaves for a week to bring out the flavour," said Esther. "Finally, we spread the seeds out and dry them in the sun before we pack them into sacks."

"That's a lot of work!" Bella exclaimed.

"You must be exhausted," Bella said with a sigh, as she helped prepare dinner in Michael and Esther's backyard.

"We are," said Esther. "But the money our community gets from the Fair Trade Company for the cocoa beans pays for all our food, school fees and medical supplies for a whole year."

"My mum buys Fair Trade chocolate," said Bella excitedly. "It's the most delicious food in the entire world, don't you think?"

"We've never tasted it," said Michael. "It's too expensive."

Bella was shocked. "But that's not fair!" she cried. "You work so hard to grow the beans that make it. Eating it is the best bit."

After all the dinner things were cleared away, Bella and the children were allowed to go out and play football.

"This is what me and my best friend Charlie do at home with our friends," Bella told Michael and Esther after the game. "After we've helped clear away the dishes, of course."

"Hurry up," squawked the Quetzal, as the light began to fade. "I can play some tricks with time but I can't stop it forever."

"I've got to go," Bella told her friends sadly. "It's my birthday tomorrow and I need to get a good night's sleep so I can help my mum get things ready for my party."

Michael glanced at his sister. Esther nodded and quickly darted away.

After all their goodbyes,
Bella and the Quetzal flew up
into the glorious night sky.

"I love finding out how other people around the world live their lives," smiled Bella happily. "And it's always amazing to see how much we have in common." It was then that she noticed the Quetzal's package.

"What's that?" she yawned.

"It's a surprise," he said with a wink.

Bella had a wonderful time at her party. Annie had made lots of delicious food and organised some great games.

"Mum, this chocolate cake is the best ever!" Bella cheered with her mouth full.

"What's that under the table?" Charlie asked.

Bella helped her mum tidy up.

"Mum," said Bella thoughtfully, "I want to send chocolate for some children in Ghana to try."

"Okay," said Annie, looking a little puzzled.

"And I want to know more about Fair Trade and where our food comes from."

It was then that Bella saw the strange oval package on the kitchen table.

"Your last present," said Annie. "I can't imagine what it could be."

Bella's heart jumped with joy. "It's chocolate!" she cried, ripping it open.

"Chocolate?" said Annie doubtfully, as she stared at the strange-looking fruit.

"Honestly, Bella, you really are full of the most delicious surprises."